Teggs is no ordinary dinosaur –
he's an **ASTROSAUR!** Captain of
the amazing spaceship DSS *Sauropod*,
he goes on dangerous missions and
fights evil – along with his faithful
crew, Gipsy, Arx and Iggy!

Collect all the **ASTROSAURS!**
Free collector cards in the back of
every book for you to swap with your
friends. More cards available
from the **ASTROSAURS** website:

www.astrosaurs.co.uk

D1150452

www.kidsatrandomhouse.co.uk

4.80

BARTER BOOKS
ALNWICK STATION
NORTHUMBERLAND

Read all the adventures of
Teggs, Gipsy, Arx and Iggy!

BOOK ONE:
RIDDLE OF THE RAPTORS

BOOK TWO:
THE HATCHING HORROR

BOOK THREE:
THE SEAS OF DOOM

Coming soon

BOOK FIVE:
THE SKIES OF FEAR

Find out more at
www.astrosaurs.co.uk

Astrosaurs

THE MIND-SWAP
MENACE

Steve Cole

Illustrated by Woody Fox

RED FOX

THE MIND-SWAP MENACE
A RED FOX BOOK 978 1 8623 0587 8

First published in Great Britain in 2005 by Red Fox,
an imprint of Random House Children's Books

5 7 9 10 8 6

Copyright © Steve Cole, 2005
Cover illustration and map © Charlie Fowkes, 2005
Illustrations copyright © Woody Fox, 2005

The right of Steve Cole to be identified as the author of this work
has been asserted in accordance with the Copyright, Designs and
Patents Act 1988.

All rights reserved. No part of this publication may be reproduced,
stored in a retrieval system, or transmitted in any form or by any
means, electronic, mechanical, photocopying, recording or otherwise,
without the prior permission of the publishers.

The Random House Group Limited supports The Forest Stewardship
Council (FSC), the leading international forest certification organisation.
All our titles that are printed on Greenpeace approved FSC certified paper
carry the FSC logo. Our paper procurement policy can be found at
www.rbooks.co.uk/environment

Mixed Sources
Product group from well-managed
forests and other controlled sources
www.fsc.org Cert no. TT-COC-2139
FSC © 1996 Forest Stewardship Council

Set in Bembo Schoolbook

Red Fox Books are published by Random House Children's Books,
61–63 Uxbridge Road, London W5 5SA,
a division of The Random House Group Ltd

Addresses for companies within The Random House Group Limited
can be found at: www.randomhouse.co.uk/offices.htm

THE RANDOM HOUSE GROUP Limited Reg. No. 954009
www.**kids**at**randomhouse**.co.uk

A CIP catalogue record for this book is available from the British Library.

Printed in the UK by CPI Bookmarque, Croydon, CR0 4TD

To Alicia

WARNING!

THINK YOU KNOW ABOUT DINOSAURS?

THINK AGAIN!

The dinosaurs . . .
Big, stupid, lumbering reptiles. Right?
All they did was eat, sleep and roar a bit. Right?
Died out millions of years ago when a big meteor struck the Earth. Right?

Wrong!

The dinosaurs weren't stupid. They may have had small brains, but they used them well. They had big thoughts and big dreams.

By the time the meteor hit, the last dinosaurs had already left Earth for ever. Some breeds had discovered how to travel through space as early as the Triassic period, and were already enjoying a new life among the stars. No one has found evidence of dinosaur technology yet. But the first fossil bones were only unearthed in 1822, and new finds are being made all the time.

The proof is out there, buried in the ground.

And the dinosaurs live on, way out in space, even now. They've settled down in a place they call the Jurassic Quadrant and over the last sixty-five million years they've gone on evolving…

The dinosaurs we'll be meeting are part of a special group called the Dinosaur Space Service. Their job is to explore space, to go on exciting missions and to fight evil and protect the innocent!

These heroic herbivores are not just dinosaurs.

They are *astrosaurs!*

NOTE: The following story has been translated from secret Dinosaur Space Service records. Earthling dinosaur names are used throughout, although some changes have been made for easy reading. There's even a guide to help you pronounce the dinosaur names at the back of the book.

THE CREW OF THE DSS SAUROPOD

**CAPTAIN
TEGGS STEGOSAUR**

ARX ORANO,
FIRST OFFICER

GIPSY SAURINE,
COMMUNICATIONS
OFFICER

IGGY TOOTH,
CHIEF ENGINEER

Jurassic Quadrant

Ankylos

Steggos

Diplox

INDEPENDEN
DINOSAUR
ALLIANCE

vegetarian sector

Squawk
Major

DSS
UNION OF
PLANETS

PTEROSAURIA

Tri System

Corytho

Lambeos

Iguanos

Aqua Minor

OUTER SPACE

Geldos Cluster

Teerex Major

Olympus

TYRANNOSAUR
TERRITORIES

carnivore
sector

Raptos

Planet Sixty

THEROPOD EMPIRE

Megalos

Cryptos

vegmeat
zone
(neutral space)

SEA REPTILE
SPACE

Pliosaur
Nurseries

Not to scale

THE MIND-SWAP MENACE

Chapter One

SPACE WRECK

The spaceship was in a hurry. Shaped like an enormous metal egg, it shot past stars and planets at top speed.

Its name was the DSS *Sauropod*. It was the fastest ship in the Dinosaur Space Service.

It was on a vital mission.

And it was about to crash at ten million miles per hour into something that shouldn't be there at all . . .

"Red alert!" squawked the alarm pterosaur, the moment she noticed. Her screeching voice echoed throughout the *Sauropod.* "Unknown object ahead! We're going to crash! *Squaaaaawk!*"

"Hit the brakes!" yelled Captain Teggs Stegosaur from his control pit. "Fast!"

His flying reptile flight crew – fifty dynamic dimorphodon – flapped into action. Their claws closed on the brake levers. Their beaks bashed at the reverse rockets.

4

The *Sauropod* spun and skidded as it screeched to a halt. Teggs — an orange-brown stegosaurus — clamped his teeth round a huge clump of ferns and held on for dear life.

"Object straight ahead!" reported Gipsy, clinging to her chair. She was a stripy hadrosaur and was in charge of the ship's communications. "Can we steer around it?"

"Not while we're spinning like this," Teggs cried. "Arx, will we stop in time?"

"It's going to be close," Arx said. He was a wise and sturdy triceratops and Teggs's second-in-command. A dozen dimorphodon grabbed hold of his horns to stop him sliding away from his controls. "Oh, no!

The brakes are burning out!"

"Don't worry, they won't let us down," cried Iggy, hanging onto a safety rail. This tough iguanodon was the *Sauropod*'s chief engineer. He knew the ship like the back of his claw. "I built those brakes myself! They can handle worse than this."

"You mean it can *get* worse than this?" cried Gipsy. Her head-crest flushed bright blue with alarm.

At last, with a final flip, the *Sauropod* came to a stop.

"I told you we'd make it," grinned Iggy.

"It was close, though," said Arx, as a dimorphodon wiped sweat from his frilly forehead.

"Switch on the scanner!" cried Teggs. "Let's see what's out there!"

More dimorphodon flocked to obey. On the screen, Teggs and his crew could see something that looked like a big, silver wheel, slowly spinning.

"Looks like a space station of some kind," said Arx.

"It's not on any of the space maps," said Gipsy. "I've sent a greetings message but there's no reply."

Teggs pointed at the screen with his spiky tail. "Maybe *that* would explain why!"

A huge, black, jagged hole had been torn in the outside of the space station.

"This is a wheel with a puncture," said Iggy. "Must be a space wreck!"

"It doesn't look very old," said Gipsy. "I wonder where it came from?"

"I don't recognize the design," said Arx. But as the wheel kept turning, he suddenly saw a blood-red sign on the silver surface. It was a dinosaur skull with rows of jagged teeth.

A shiver crept up the long, bony spines of the astrosaurs. They all knew that this design was the mark of meat-eaters.

"It's a carnivore space station!" cried Iggy. "What's it doing here in the Vegetarian Sector?"

"It could be a trick," Gipsy suggested. "Maybe some meat-eaters are sneakily trying to invade us."

"There are no other ships nearby," said Arx. "It's more likely that this wreck has just drifted across from their side of space into ours."

"Well, we can't just leave it here," said Teggs. "It's a danger to passing ships. Let's zip across and set up a beacon there, like a lighthouse in space, warning other travellers away."

Arx cleared his scaly throat. "Excuse me, sir, but can we spare the time? We *are* in the middle of a mercy mission."

Teggs had not forgotten. On the planet Diplos, whole herds of starving diplodocus needed help fast. A freak hailstorm had wiped out their harvest.

The *Sauropod* had been loaded up with plants and seeds so the dinosaurs could feed again.

"I think this is important, Arx," said Teggs. "What if *another* ship on *another* important mission crashes into this thing? That could lead to total disaster!"

Arx bowed his head. "You're quite right, Captain," he said. "I'm sorry."

"Nothing to be sorry about," smiled Teggs. "Now, I'd better go and get the beacon."

"I'll get the shuttle ready!" said Iggy, bounding off to the lift.

Teggs reared up out of the control pit. "We won't be long. Warm up the engines and be ready to zoom off to Diplos the moment we're back on board."

"We'll be ready, sir," Gipsy promised.

Arx said nothing, his eyes glued to the scanner screen. He wished Teggs

and Iggy didn't have to go. He had a
niggling feeling in his bones that this
sinister space wreck spelled danger.

It took less than a minute for the
shuttle to reach the space station. Teggs
and Iggy climbed in through the air
lock. They found themselves in a
gloomy corridor.

"Let's have a quick look around," said
Teggs. "Just in case anyone has been
hurt."

"If there are any meat-eaters still on
this station, *we* could get hurt!" said
Iggy. Even so, he followed his captain

along the dark passage without hesitation.

The station was a grim, forbidding place. It was made of metal and thick with shadows. To their right, stars shone a ghostly light through small, barred windows in the outer wall. To their left was a line of heavy doors, covered in bolts and locks.

Teggs tried one of them. The door creaked open onto a cramped room with just a bed and a bucket inside. It looked like some kind of jail cell.

"Iggy? I think this place was a prison," said Teggs. "A lockup for carnivore criminals!"

Iggy agreed. "Pretty *dangerous* criminals, too, from the size of those locks!"

"We won't hang about," said Teggs. "Let's get the beacon working and go back to the *Sauropod*."

Iggy took the bulky beacon from his

13

captain's back and set it up in the cell.
It looked like a large red triangle with
a transmitter on the top.

"There," said Iggy. "That will send
out a recorded message telling any
passing ships to keep out of the way."

Teggs grinned at him. "Next stop,
Diplos! Come on."

But the cell door wouldn't open.

"Funny," said Teggs. "Must be stuck."

"But we left it open so we could
move about!" Iggy remembered.
"There's hardly room in

here to swing a compsognathus!"

Teggs nodded grimly. "So either it swung shut behind us and jammed – or someone has locked us in!"

A nasty snigger came from the other side of the door. Then a white, wispy gas started pumping through the keyhole.

"Hold your breath, Iggy!" Teggs gasped. "We've walked into a trap!"

Chapter Two

THE MIND-SWAPPER

"It's too late, Captain," choked Iggy, clutching at his throat as the gas engulfed him. "I'm getting dizzy . . ." He fell face-first onto the ground, his short, stiff tail pointing up in the air.

Teggs bashed his body against the

door with all his strength. But it was no good. The door was too strong, and the gas was making him weak.

As he slipped to the floor beside Iggy, he rolled over and squashed the beacon flat.

Gipsy had been listening to the beacon's signal. "The warning's coming out loud and clear," she told Arx, happily.

But then the signal stopped dead.

"What happened?" asked Arx.

"I don't know," said Gipsy. "Maybe the beacon is faulty." She tried to get Teggs on the communicator. "Captain Teggs, this is Gipsy. Is everything OK?"

There was no reply.

"Come on, Gipsy," said Arx. "Let's get over there. I've got a bad feeling about that place."

Gipsy told the dimorphodon to look after the control room until they returned, then followed Arx over to the lift. "You think Teggs and Iggy could be in trouble, don't you?"

"I only hope I'm wrong," sighed Arx.

But Gipsy knew that Arx was rarely wrong about anything.

Slowly, Teggs woke up. He ached from the tip of his tail to the bottom of his beak. His head felt like it was full of extra-smelly dung, and his mouth was as dry as a desert.

He opened his eyes to find himself lying on his side in a large, well-lit room. A big TV buzzed in the corner, its screen full of static. How did he get there?

Suddenly he remembered the gas, and the evil snigger from behind the cell door.

"Iggy!" he cried. "Iggy, are you all right?"

"I think so," gasped Iggy weakly from somewhere behind him. "But I can't move!"

Teggs tried to kick his legs. "I can't move either. I've been tied up!"

"You have indeed, you pair of plant-eating potatoes," said a sinister voice nearby. "My home-made sleep

gas made it easy-peasy. You are now in my power! Aren't they, Ardul?"

"Yes, sir, Mr Boss." This second voice sounded altogether more stupid. "They is in your clutches, and that is the truth."

"What do you want with us?" Teggs demanded, struggling to free his legs. "Who are you? Where are we?"

There was a quiet thud and a scampering sound. Suddenly, a mean little dinosaur with goblin eyes and rows of sharp teeth was standing over Teggs's head. "Good afternoon," he hissed. "You are in the prison officers' lounge."

"Are you prison officers, then?" Teggs asked.

"We used to be *prisoners* – but soon we shall be free dinosaurs again!" The mean little meat-eater chuckled and his thick friend quickly joined in. "My name is Dasta – Crool Dasta, the sneakiest coelophysis ever!"

"Crool Dasta?!" gasped Teggs.

Dasta flashed an evil smile. "You've heard of me, then?"

"No," Teggs admitted. "I just can't believe you've got such a stupid name."

"I happen to be an evil inventor and a criminal genius," said Dasta snootily.

"You can't be *that* clever," said Teggs. "Otherwise you wouldn't have been caught! Or did your stupid sidekick mess things up for you?"

At that, Ardul came running up to him. Ardul was another coelophysis – shorter, fatter and twice as ugly as his boss.

"Don't speak to us that way," said Ardul. "You is dating on thin ice."

"You mean *skating* on thin ice, Ardul," sighed Dasta.

"Where's everyone else?" Iggy asked.

"This prison was almost destroyed when a meteor crashed into it," hissed Dasta. "Everyone else got away. The prison officers thought that Ardul and I were killed in the explosion — but we were only hiding!"

"Neat trick," said Teggs. "How long have you been hanging out on this space wreck?"

"Three months," the carnivore confessed. "But I knew that one day we would drift into the path of another ship — and we would be free once more! Free to collect our secret treasure from the Geldos Cluster and live like kings!"

"Free?" Teggs scoffed. "Come off it.

You may have caught us, but you're still stuck here."

"I don't think so," sniggered Dasta. "Your crew will be getting worried. They will come to get you. But what they'll get is *us*, Ardul and me — and they won't even know it!"

Teggs felt worried all of a sudden. "What are you talking about?"

"Take a look at your ugly friend and find out," Dasta snorted.

Teggs rolled over backwards to see. "Iggy!" he cried. "You're wearing some weird contraption on your head!"

"So are *you*, Captain," said Iggy nervously.

Dasta gave a gurgling laugh. Then he placed a similar helmet on his own head. Ardul did the same.

"The helmets are connected to my latest brilliant invention," Dasta explained, pointing to a menacing machine full of buttons and coloured lights. "It's a mind-swapper! It will put my brain in your body, Captain Teggs, and Ardul's brain into Iggy's!"

Teggs gulped. "What happens to *our* brains?"

"They is gonna be sucked into *our* bodies," said Ardul, with a cruel grin.

"We shall become you," hissed Dasta.

"And
you shall become us!
Your foolish friends will take
us back to your ship – and we'll take
over!"

"No!" cried Teggs.

"Yes," laughed Dasta. "Ardul, start the
machine!"

The mind-swapper began to throb
and hiss and steam. Blue electric light
crackled all around it. Then it made
a nasty sucking noise, like a slug

trying to swallow a boiled sweet.

Teggs cried out. His brain felt on fire.
Dasta laughed and clapped as the
machine sucked harder and harder . . .

Chapter Three

STRANDED IN SPACE

With a loud POP! it was all over.

Teggs found he could move.
Confused, he got to his feet. But he
was no longer a massive, powerful,
seven-ton stegosaur. Now he was a
zippy, nippy little monster, as light as a
feather. His mind had been plopped
into Dasta's body!

And Dasta, meanwhile had taken Teggs's form. "My invention works perfectly!" he cried. "Everyone will think I'm Captain Teggs of the DSS!"

"Iggy?" the real Teggs asked. His voice came out as a nasty little hiss. "Iggy, tell me you're still you!"

But his old friend only sniggered. "I is not Iggy!" he said. "I is Ardul!"

"His mind's taken over my body, Captain," said the real Iggy. "While

I'm stuck as the ugliest coelophysis in the galaxy! What are we going to do?"

"We have to reverse the mind-swap!" cried Teggs. "They're still tied up, they can't stop us!"

"Only *I* can swap our minds back again," jeered Dasta. "You'll never work out how it's done!"

Teggs stared at the controls and tried to think. But being in someone else's body was very distracting. He clicked his long, pointed claws together. He ran his tongue over his sharp teeth – and nearly sliced it off. There was a horrible taste in his mouth – raw meat! He was almost sick at the thought of it.

Suddenly the door burst open, and Gipsy and Arx rushed in.

"Arx! Gipsy!" cried the real Teggs in delight. "You're here!"

Gipsy frowned. "Who in space are *you*?"

"You wicked little meat-eaters," snarled Arx. "How dare you tie up our friends!"

"*We're* your friends!" wailed the real Iggy, jumping up and down in his bogus body. "Not them!"

But Arx and Gipsy ignored him. Straight away, they started untying the *fake* Teggs and Iggy!

"Please, listen!" the real Teggs begged them in his new, hissy voice. "We may look like mean carnivores, but I'm really your captain – and he is the real Iggy! Our minds have been put in the wrong bodies, that's all!"

"Ridiculous!" cried Dasta. "What a silly story."

And Arx believed him, of course, because he looked and sounded just like Teggs.

"Now come on, Arx, get your beak

moving on those ropes. Ahhh!" Dasta winked at the real Teggs. "Free at last!"

"That is better!" cried Ardul, as Gipsy untied his ropes and he got to his feet. "*Much* better!"

"You're making a big mistake!" cried the real Teggs. "Arx, *please*—"

But before he could say anything else, Dasta lashed out with his long stegosaur tail – and sent him flying into the real Iggy. Both the little dinosaurs ended up in a dazed heap in the corner.

Dasta chuckled. He liked this new body — it was full of power!

"Was that necessary, Captain?" Arx frowned.

"Don't feel sorry for him," said the fake Teggs. "That's Crool Dasta — the cleverest crook in the cosmos. I expect you've heard of me. Er . . . him. Haven't you?"

"No," said Arx.

Dasta sighed. "Well, anyway, he and his friend have been stuck on this space wreck for months, and it must have turned their brains funny. All this talk of swapping minds and bodies . . . Ha!"

"What does this gadget do?" asked Gipsy, pointing to the mind-swapper.

"It's a terrible torture device," Dasta lied. "First, they gassed us. Then they tied us up. If you hadn't saved us, I don't know *what* would have happened." He reared up, eager to be off. "Now come on, we must be going!"

Arx frowned. "Don't you want to set up another beacon here?"

"No time!" he cried. "We're in a rush!"

"Very well," said Arx. "I suppose we'd better take these crooks with us. We can drop them off at DSS Headquarters on our way back from Diplos."

"This pair aren't going anywhere," said Dasta. "Deal with them, er . . . Iggy?"

The fake Iggy marched over to the little dinosaurs and grabbed them by their tails. Then he shoved them both down the rubbish chute! A moment later, the mind-swap machine was stuffed down after them.

"Iggy, what are you doing!" cried Gipsy. "Whatever they've done, we can't just leave those dinosaurs here!"

"Of course we can," said Dasta.

"Now, lead the way back to our ship.
And that's an order!"

Arx nodded slowly. "Yes, Captain."

As Arx and Gipsy led the way, Dasta
turned to Ardul. "I think I'm going to
enjoy being a spaceship captain," he
hissed. "From now on, my mind is

staying in *this* body."

"I is gonna enjoy being an iggu-nana, too," said Ardul. "But I is not liking the thought of eating plants."

Dasta sniggered. "When these fools have taken us to the Geldos Cluster, they'll be of no more use to us." He licked his new, stegosaurus lips. "And then we'll eat the lot of them!"

Sprawled on a big heap of rubbish, the real Teggs opened his eyes. All around was dark and slimy and stank of rotten meat.

"Iggy?" he hissed. "Are you there?"

There was a clattering from the pile beside him. "Just about," Iggy groaned.

"I've never been hit by my own tail before," said Teggs, ruefully. "That body of mine packs quite a punch, doesn't it!"

"What are we going to do, Captain?" Iggy whispered.

Teggs reached out a claw and patted him on the shoulder. "Don't worry," he said. "We'll find a way out of this."

But then, a deep rumbling sounded from the darkness. The rotten rubbish they were sitting on started to tremble and shake.

Teggs stared around blindly. "What's that?"

"I'd know that noise anywhere," said Iggy. "It's engines. The *Sauropod* shuttle's engines!"

"Then . . ." Teggs swallowed, "then they're leaving us behind!"

"We'll never see our friends again," said Iggy, sadly. "And we'll *never* get our bodies back!"

Chapter Four

NO ESCAPE

Dasta enjoyed the walk from the
Sauropod's shuttle bay to the flight deck.
Everyone he passed thought he was
really Teggs, and they all smiled and
saluted. Clearly, Teggs was a popular
captain.

"He won't be for much longer,"
chuckled Dasta.

Gipsy and Arx led him on to the flight deck. Ardul was right behind him. Unfortunately, he was finding it harder than Dasta to get used to his new body. He kept walking into doors and walls.

"Iggy, mind out!" said Gipsy. "You'll bring the whole place crashing down."

"I is just, um, a bit dizzy after breathing in the grass," said Ardul.

"*Gas*, you idiot!" cried Dasta. "They didn't leave us on a lawn, did they?"

"If you're not feeling well, Iggy, maybe you should lie down in your room," Arx suggested.

"Sounds good," said Ardul. "Where *is* my room?"

Gipsy frowned. "I'll get one of the dimorphodon to take you there. Try to get some sleep!"

She whistled to a dimorphodon and it flapped off into the lift. Ardul followed, drooling.

"Don't eat it, you idiot," whispered Dasta. "Or they'll know for sure you aren't the real Iggy!"

"It is a juicy looking flapper," sighed Ardul, as the lift doors closed behind him. "But I will try."

"Ready to go, Captain," said Arx. "Full speed ahead to Diplos?"

"Diplos? Get real!" Dasta snorted. He stumbled into Teggs's control pit and tried to look natural. "Steer this ship to the Geldos Cluster."

"Geldos?" Arx blinked. "But that's in meat-eater space!"

"So?"

"So, we're plant-eaters!" Gipsy protested. "We can't just enter the Carnivore Sector without permission! They might think we are invading!"

"Well, we'll worry about that when the time comes," said Dasta. "Head for the Geldos Cluster – now!"

"Why?" asked Arx. "What's so important? What about all those poor dinosaurs starving on Diplos?"

Dasta peered at him from the pit. "Who is your captain, Arx?" he said quietly.

Arx stiffened. "*You* are, sir."

"Then do as I say, you tiresome triceratops!" he bellowed. "Now!"

Gipsy felt her legs wobble as Arx changed the *Sauropod's* course through space. She had never, ever heard Teggs shout at his first officer before. What was the matter with him? Could the gas have affected him more than they'd thought?

Teggs was acting like a totally different dinosaur . . .

★

Back on the prison, the real Teggs and Iggy were trying to find their way out of the slippery, slimy rubbish heap, carefully carrying the mind-swapper. They moved slowly at first, not used to their new, unfamiliar bodies. But soon they were climbing nimbly through the rubbish pile towards a faint, ghostly light.

"Where's it coming from?" asked Iggy.

"It's coming from the end of this chute," Teggs reported. He patted a filthy metal pipe. "If we can climb up this thing, we'll reach that light."

"What does it matter?" sighed Iggy. "We're trapped here for ever, inside these silly little bodies – while Dasta and Ardul lead the *Sauropod* off to find their secret treasure!"

"We'll get our bodies back," said Teggs. "After all, we've still got the mind-swapper. There's still hope!"

After a lot of scrabbling about, they found themselves at the top of the rubbish chute. A glass lid blocked their way out but

Teggs found he was able to use his claws to prise it open.

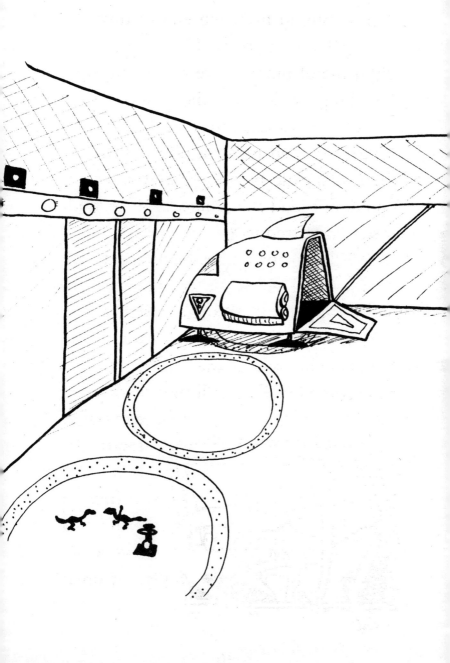

Iggy crawled out after him, carrying the mind-swap machine. "Where are we now?" he asked.

Teggs looked around. They were in a large, echoing chamber, which was dimly lit by a single light bulb. It was empty except for one thing – a spaceship.

"This must be the prison's docking bay!" cried Teggs. "When everyone else evacuated, I guess that ship wasn't needed – so it was left behind!"

"Maybe it doesn't work," said Iggy, trying not to get too excited.

"You'll soon get it going again," Teggs told him. "You're brilliant with engines!"

The two of them ran across the deserted shuttle bay to inspect the ship.

"It looks all right," said Iggy. "Tip-top, in fact. Which strikes me as strange."

"Why?" asked Teggs.

"Well, Dasta's clever with machines too," he said. "So why didn't he just get on this ship with Ardul and take off for the Geldos Cluster months ago?"

"Maybe he didn't know it was here," Teggs argued, climbing up the steps to the spaceship. He threw open the door.

And an ear-splitting alarm went off.

"Maybe!" gasped Iggy. "Or maybe he knew *that* would happen!"

"So what!" said Teggs. "It's only an alarm. There's no one left to hear it!"

But Teggs was wrong.

A hidden door in the wall slid open. And something truly terrifying came out.

Clanking and steaming, a line of massive mechanical T. rexes trooped into the docking bay. Each one was the size of a *Sauropod* shuttle. Their red laser eyes swept all about the room.

"Now we know why Dasta and Ardul didn't take this ship," gasped Iggy. "The prison officers must use these things as guards!"

"Just as scary as real T. rexes," Teggs agreed. "But much easier to train, and

less likely to eat the crooks they're
guarding!"

"*Prisoners escaping,*" said the robot T.
rex leader in a jerky voice. "*Prisoners
identified as Dasta and Ardul.*"

"We're not!" shouted Teggs. "We're
peaceful astrosaurs! We're just trapped
in their rotten bodies!"

51

But the computerized carnivores weren't listening. They started clanking towards the shuttle. "*Escaping prisoners must be destroyed!*" they roared. "*Kill them! Kill them both!*"

Teggs and Iggy stared helplessly as the T. rex robots closed in.

Chapter Five

THE ENEMY WITHIN

"Look out!" yelled Teggs, as the nearest robot T. rex fired laser beams from its glowing eyes. He grabbed Iggy by the arm and dragged him out of the way. The blast struck the side of the ship, which went up in smoke.

"Thanks, Teggs!" said Iggy. "That was close!"

"We've got one tiny chance," Teggs said. "Our new bodies are smaller and faster than our normal ones. That'll make us harder to hit."

Another blast of ruby light burned into the ground beside them. Teggs and

Iggy ran for their lives, zigzagging across the floor. But more and more laser beams came zapping from the

metal creatures' eyes.

"We can't dodge them for ever!" gasped Iggy.

Teggs nodded, and felt the searing heat of a death ray sizzle past his head. "Change of plan. Follow me!"

To Iggy's amazement, Teggs sprinted *towards* the nearest killer robot! He ducked in and out of the monster's massive metal feet. Terrified, Iggy ran after him and joined in the dangerous dance.

"It can't shoot us when we're almost underneath it," Teggs explained.

"But its friends can!" cried Iggy. Even now, more robots were closing in.

"Get ready to dodge when I do," Teggs told him. "NOW!"

He and Iggy ducked away from the robot's legs just as four of the T. rexes opened fire. The blast blew up the creature's ankles. With a great robotic roar, it crashed to the ground.

"One down, seven to go!" gasped Teggs. "We have to stay ahead of them!"

Suddenly, Iggy had an idea. "Or just *stay on their heads*!" he shouted. "What do you think? These little bodies of ours should be good for climbing."

"I'm game if you are," said Teggs.

Together, they darted over to the nearest robot. It tried to stamp on them, but they were too fast and jumped on its tail. It tried to shake them off, but they were already climbing up its mechanical backbone.

"Why are we heading for the head?" asked Teggs.

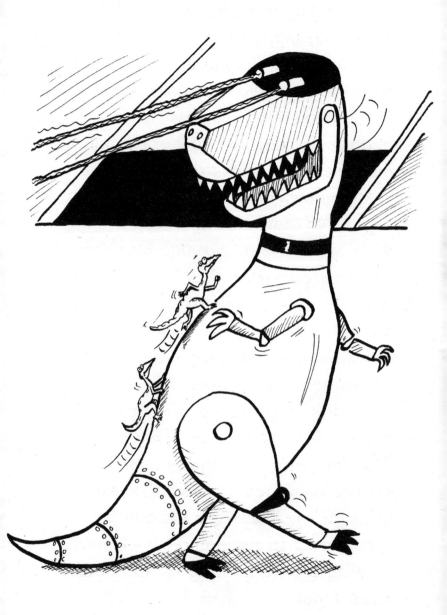

"I want to do some robot brain surgery!" Iggy smiled. "This mind swap has put me in the mood!" And he dug his coelophysis claws into the back of the robot's head. A moment later he had ripped away a metal panel and pulled out the wires within.

The robot bucked like a deranged donkey, trying to shake them off. Teggs and Iggy clung on for dear life.

"What are you trying to do?" Teggs yelled.

"Start a brainstorm," Iggy explained, wiggling some wires. "With any luck, this thing won't just be after us any more. It'll be after anything that moves!"

There was a flash from inside the robot's metal head. Suddenly, it was firing its lasers at the other T. rexes! One burst into flames and crashed against its neighbour, bringing it burning to the ground. The other

T. rexes fired back wildly, hitting each other as well as the rebel robot. Their metal bodies were soon scorched and smoking. One by one they exploded in a blaze of sparks and went crashing to the ground.

When the chaos was over, Teggs and Iggy were still clinging to their rebel-robot's scrambled circuits. It looked around for anything else to

fight – but found nothing. Slowly, the
lights in its eyes flickered out. Then, it
began to sway from side to side.

"Get ready to jump!" cried Teggs, as
the robot finally toppled over.

At the last possible moment, he and
Iggy jumped clear. The robot smashed
into the ground – and they skidded

safely on their bottoms to the far side of the smoky shuttle bay.

"We made it!" whooped Iggy. "We actually made it!"

"We did," Teggs agreed. "But I'm not sure the ship was so lucky!"

Iggy's smile soon vanished as the smoke started to clear. Now he could see that the shuttle had been well and truly zapped. It had more holes in it than a Swiss cheese.

"I hope you can fix that ship, Iggy," said Teggs. "Because if you can't, we'll be stuck here for good!"

Gipsy was worried. Her captain was acting very strangely. First, he ordered them to fly into the Carnivore Sector. Then he said he was going off to take a nap. Teggs *never* napped on duty.

While Arx sat at his controls in a sulk, Gipsy decided to visit Iggy. She would ask him *exactly* what happened

on board the space wreck. Perhaps he
would remember something that might
explain Teggs's odd behaviour.

But as she neared Iggy's room, she
stopped. She could hear voices. Teggs
was in there, talking to Iggy. He wasn't
having a nap at all!

Gipsy pressed her ear up against the
door.

"We'll be coming up to the
Carnivore Sector any time now," Teggs
was saying. "From there, it should only

take a few hours to reach Geldos."

"I isn't thinking I can last that long!"
Iggy roared.

Why was he talking so strangely?
Gipsy wondered.

"I is needing fresh meat! Let me eat
just one of them flappers."

"No!" said Teggs.

"There is lots of them about! No one
will miss just one!"

"I said no! You're supposed to be an
iguanodon. Eat some more ferns."

"Ferns taste of poo," Iggy grumbled.
"Can't we just get *one* flapper? I will
only nibble its beak, promise!"

Gipsy gasped and jumped away from

the door. Something was *very* wrong. Just what had happened to Teggs and Iggy on that space wreck?

She rushed back to the flight deck. She would tell Arx. Maybe *he* would know what to do.

But Arx had problems of his own.

The *Sauropod* had been in the Carnivore Sector  less than two minutes when a scary ship came whizzing into view. It was blood-red and shaped like a huge, jagged tooth, gleaming in the starlight.

"A raptor death ship," breathed Arx. It was the biggest he'd ever seen. He jabbed the red alert button with his nose horn and the alarm pterosaur started squawking wildly.

"Captain Teggs, Gipsy, this is Arx. Please report to the flight deck! Iggy, get to the engine room, quick!"

Gipsy arrived seconds later. "I was just on my way to see you," she said. "What's up?" Then she saw the death ship on the scanner and her head-crest flushed bright blue. "Arx, they're sending us a message!"

"I suppose we'd better hear it then," said Arx gravely.

Gipsy flicked a switch. A sinister hissing voice sounded from the  speakers. "Thisss is the Raptor Border Patrol," it said. "You have entered the Carnivore Sssector without permission. Prepare to be destroyed!"

Chapter Six

CHASE THROUGH SPACE

The dimorphodon flapped about in alarm. Arx swallowed hard. "This is the DSS *Sauropod*," he said. "Please do not open fire. We are here on an urgent mission! At least, I *think* it's urgent."

"What isss thisss mission?" demanded the raptors.

Arx turned to Gipsy helplessly. "What do I tell them? I don't know *what* we're doing here!"

Suddenly the lift doors opened and Teggs appeared – or rather, Dasta appeared in Teggs's body. "Why the red alert?" he asked.

"We're about to be blown up by a raptor death ship, Captain," said Arx. "They want to know what we're doing here."

"Stupid raptors, sticking their snouts in," said Dasta. "It's none of their business!"

"*We* would like to know too," Gipsy said firmly.

"How dare you question your own captain?" Dasta roared. "Now let's just blast these raptors and get on with it!"

Arx stared at him in horror. "We can't just open fire on a raptor border patrol! That is an act of war!"

"And disobeying me is *mutiny*, Arx!" said Dasta. "Fire cannons, torpedoes, everything. All at once!"

Arx rushed over to the fake Teggs, still unaware that an evil carnivore had borrowed his captain's body. "Please, Captain," he said. "It's not called a death ship for nothing! They could destroy us!"

"Thisss isss your last chance," hissed the raptors through the *Sauropod*'s speakers. "Explain yourselves or die!"

"We have to fire first," said Dasta. He gave Arx a crafty smile. "Trust me, Arx. Have I ever let you down before?"

"No," Arx admitted. "Never."

He wanted to believe in his captain, more than anything.

Gipsy waited nervously. Would Arx do what he was told?

At last, he told the dimorphodon: "Very well. Fire everything as the captain says."

The flying reptiles flapped off to obey. They fired lasers, cannons and dung torpedoes. The death ship shook and lurched to one side as the weapons found their mark.

But then it straightened up, and started speeding towards them.

"Was that the best we could do?" complained Dasta. "Rubbish!"

"Plant-eating ssscum!" the raptors hissed. "Prepare to die!"

"Well, if we can't shoot them down, we'd better run!" said Dasta grumpily. "But stay on course for Geldos!"

"Full speed ahead!" shouted Arx.

The *Sauropod* sped away. But the death ship was right behind them. It opened fire, and the *Sauropod* rocked with the blast.

"They've blown off our lasers!" said Arx.

"They're gaining on us!" cried Gipsy.

"Go faster!" snapped Dasta.

"We can't!" Arx said. "Not unless Iggy boosts the engines!"

"I'll call him," said Gipsy. She flicked
a switch. "Iggy? Iggy, we need you to
boost the engines!"

"Hang on, stripy girl." It sounded like
Iggy, but of course it was really Ardul.
"I is just trying to find the engine
room."

"Iggy, what's wrong with you?" she
wailed.

"I is fine," he said. "But what does an
engine look like again?"

Arx frowned. "He's gone crazy!"

"Just a touch of brain flu," said
Dasta. "He's been looking a bit peaky
lately, don't you think?"

"Well, Captain," said Gipsy coldly. "I certainly noticed he wasn't himself."

The *Sauropod* shook as another blast hit home.

"Our cannons have been hit!" cried Gipsy.

"There's just one chance!" Arx shouted. "Perhaps if we dump all our dung torpedoes . . ."

"*Dump* them?" Dasta roared. "That will leave us at their mercy!"

"Not if we dump them right in their path!" grinned Gipsy.

"Exactly," said Arx. "Let's do it."

Gipsy whistled at the dimorphodon. They flapped off eagerly and set to work.

"Ready for dumping . . . now!" cried Gipsy.

Arx hit a button, and fifty dung torpedoes dropped out of the *Sauropod's* bottom.

The raptor death ship was going too

fast to stop. It flew right into the astrosaurs' trap! The torpedoes all went off together in one big bang . . .

And when it was over, the death ship had become a *dung* ship! It no longer looked like a big, scary tooth – just a massive, smelly dung ball!

The dimorphodon clapped and cheered, and Gipsy slapped Arx on the back proudly.

"That should slow the raptors down," she said. "Good thinking, Arx."

"Yes, well," said Dasta sniffily. "A very clever plan, I'm sure."

"You should know, Captain," said Arx. "You *invented* that plan."

Dasta gulped. "I did?"

"Yes, in your final space exam," said Arx, advancing slowly. "Admiral Rosso was so impressed by your quick thinking, he made you the captain of the *Sauropod* straight away."

"Or rather, he made *Teggs* the captain of the *Sauropod*," said Gipsy. "But you're *not* Teggs, are you? Just like Iggy isn't Iggy. You're both imposters!"

"Nonsense, girl!" snarled Dasta. "Of course I'm Teggs! You must be spacesick!"

"The real Teggs would never have risked our lives like that," Gipsy argued. "And the real Iggy knows what an engine looks like!"

"You've been acting funny ever since we rescued you," said Arx. "At first I thought that the gas on the space prison had made you ill. But now I think you must actually be Crool Dasta and his sidekick. You have put your minds in the bodies of our friends!"

"You're crazy!" cried Dasta.

"It explains a lot," said Gipsy. "I heard them talking in Iggy's room, Arx. They were talking about eating the dimorphodon!"

At this, the dimorphodon shrieked and cheeped and fluttered.

"Why would we want to eat them?" Dasta protested. "There's not enough meat on them!"

75

Arx and Gipsy gasped in horror.
Dasta realized he had said too much.

"So, *that's* why Iggy stuck those two
coelophysis down the rubbish chute,"
said Gipsy. "To stop them convincing us
of who you really were! Those nasty
little dinosaurs used to be *you*, before
you swapped minds. Now they're Teggs
and Iggy!"

"Well done, you sap-swallowing
fools!" The fake Teggs jumped out of the

control pit. "You worked it out at last. I *am* the one and only Crool Dasta!"

"Then I'm turning round, right now," said Arx.

"No!" Dasta cried.

"Yes," Arx insisted. "The starving dinosaurs of Diplos *need* the food we're carrying. We'll rescue the real Teggs and Iggy on the way."

"And then you are going to put their minds back in their own bodies," Gipsy warned Dasta. "Or else!"

Just then, the lift doors opened and Ardul came out. "Is this the engine room?" he asked.

"Never mind that, Ardul!" snapped Dasta. "Grab the girl!"

Gipsy gasped as the fake Iggy
yanked her arm.

"Let her go!" said Arx. He lowered
his head, ready to charge.

"Stay back," hissed Dasta. "Or we'll
do something *very* nasty to your
friend. Come on, Ardul, let's get out of
here."

"Yes, sir, Mr Boss-Captain," said
Ardul. He bundled Gipsy into the lift.

"Go ahead and turn this ship round,
Arx," Dasta cried. "We'll take a shuttle
to Geldos from here. And if you try to

stop us, you'll never see Gipsy again!"
He squeezed into the lift behind them
and cackled with glee. "I've won!
Nothing in the universe can stop me
now!"

Chapter Seven

THE TREASURE OF GELDOS

Gipsy tried to escape, but Ardul's grip was too strong. Dasta led them to the nearest shuttle and she was thrown inside.

"Why are you doing all this?" she demanded, rubbing her bruised arm.

"What is so important about the Geldos Cluster?"

"A great treasure is hidden there," said Dasta. He started the shuttle's engines. "The most valuable invention in the world!"

"Invented by you?"

"Of course!" he snapped. "Before Ardul and I were arrested, I managed to hide it on a tiny planet in the middle of the Cluster."

"What were you arrested for, anyway?" asked Gipsy.

"My invention was very expensive to build," said Dasta. "I had to rob the Universal Raptor Bank to pay for the parts. That's why I teamed up with Ardul."

Ardul nodded proudly. "I is the best rank slobber in space."

81

"The best *bank robber*, you dino-nut. And I only wish you were!" The shuttle took off in a cloud of stinky smoke. "Ardul here forgot to wear his robber's mask," Dasta explained. "He was recognized. The raptor police tracked him down – and me with him!"

"Good," said Gipsy. But she had to admit she was curious. "What *is* this incredible invention, anyway?"

"The replicator," said Dasta proudly. "It makes a perfect copy of anything you put inside it. Gold . . . jewels . . . anything at all!"

Gipsy gasped. "That *is* amazing!"

Dasta pulled a gold piece from his belt. "All I need is a single coin, and I can make a million more . . ."

"That is what you is promising to pay me for slobbing that rank," grumbled Ardul. "One million gold pieces."

"And that's what you shall get, my friend," said Dasta. "When the replicator is mine once again!"

"So where exactly did you hide it?" Gipsy asked.

"On Geldos Beta," said Dasta. He

peered at the shuttle's controls. "In this little tub, we should reach there in just over two hours!"

Gipsy glanced down at her communicator. What Dasta didn't know was that she had secretly switched it on. Every word of their conversation had been transmitted to Arx back on the *Sauropod*.

But was there anything Arx could do?

★

On the flight deck, Arx listened gravely to Dasta's boasting. The dimorphodon were perched all over him, twittering and flapping in dismay. Arx was glad of their company. With Teggs, Iggy and Gipsy all lost and in danger, he felt very lonely indeed.

"What we need is a plan," he said, gruffly, pulling himself together. "Any ideas?"

"Eep," said a dimorphodon.

"That's correct," Arx said. "We know where they're going – Geldos Beta."

"Eep, eep," said another.

"Yes, we *can* go faster than they can, so we could get there first," he agreed. "But then what?" He sighed. "Do I dare risk a rescue? If I mess things up, Gipsy could get hurt. Oh, if only the real Teggs and Iggy were here!"

A dimorphodon flapped down and

patted him on the horn with a sympathetic wing.

But then two more of the reptiles squawked. Arx looked up sharply. The sensors were showing a ship close by. "Turn on the scanners!" he barked.

On the screen, Arx could see a small, dark ship approaching. Picked out in red on the side of the craft was a now-familiar dinosaur skull with rows of jagged teeth.

"It's a meat-eater ship," breathed Arx. "And we have no weapons. If they

attack us, we can't fight back!"

The dimorphodon squawked in alarm. Arx started to sweat as the ship drew closer.

"What can I do?" he wailed. "If I run, it means running out on Gipsy. But if I stay, the *Sauropod* could be destroyed. And then the starving dinosaurs on Diplos will *never* get their food in time!"

There was no doubt about it. The carnivore craft was heading straight for the *Sauropod*.

Chapter Eight

DOUBLE-CROSSED!

Arx waited for the approaching ship to ask what he was doing in meat-eater space. He fully expected the rasp of a raptor or the grating roar of a T. rex to sound over the *Sauropod*'s speakers.

But the speakers stayed silent. Had they been damaged in the fight with the death ship?

"If they won't talk to me, I'll have to talk to them," Arx decided. He pressed a button. "Calling carnivore ship.

This is Arx Orano of the DSS *Sauropod*. Can you hear me?"

The ship made no response.

"We are plant-eaters and mean you no harm," said Arx. "We were brought here against our wishes by wanted carnivore criminals. It's a long story. First, we lost our captain and our chief engineer—"

"Cheer up, Arx!" came a hissing voice from the speakers. "You've just found them again!"

"What?" Arx frowned. "Who is this?"

"It's Teggs!" cried the creepy voice.

"And Iggy!" came another, more stupid-sounding voice. "We just worked out how to turn on the communicator!"

"What's happening, Arx?" asked Teggs. "I knew you'd soon see through that dastardly Dasta and his stupid sidekick!"

"Not soon enough, I'm afraid,"

sighed Arx. "Come on board, Captain. I'll tell you all about it!"

Fifteen minutes later, Teggs was back in his control pit. He ran around eating all the ferns he could reach.

Arx looked down at him fondly. "I'm glad to see that whatever body you're in, your stomach remains the same size!"

Teggs grinned up at him. "Just trying to get the taste of smelly old meat out of this mouth," he said. "Hey, Iggy, jump in. Plenty of plants for us both in here!"

"Incoming!" whooped Iggy, as he dived to join him.

Arx noticed that the dimorphodon were hanging back. They just couldn't believe that these two nasty-looking meat-eaters were actually Teggs and Iggy. But Arx could, now that he'd seen them up close. He could see the friendly sparkle in their eyes. However they looked, that would always stay the same.

"Now then, Arx," Teggs said with a belch. "Let's swap stories."

Teggs told of how he and Iggy had managed to escape rubbish chutes and robots . . . How Iggy had managed to repair the only remaining ship . . . And how they had taken the mind-swapper and headed straight for the Geldos Cluster. They knew Dasta and Ardul would go there, and planned to get their bodies back!

Arx told Teggs of the *Sauropod's* dangerous journey – and of the one that Gipsy was making even as they spoke. He also explained about Dasta's treasure.

"A replicator?" Iggy frowned. "I don't believe it!"

Arx shrugged. "I wouldn't have believed that a mind-swapping machine was possible – but I'm looking at the proof!"

"Not for much longer, I hope," said Teggs. "Somehow we have to fix Dasta and Ardul for good, set Gipsy free, and swap back into our own bodies."

"And *then* take all those plants and

seeds we're carrying straight to Diplos!"
added Arx.

"Is that all?" sighed Iggy. "What shall
we do *after* breakfast?"

"Have an early lunch!" Teggs winked
at him. "Arx, if we travel at top speed,
can we still get to Geldos Beta ahead
of Dasta in the shuttle?"

Arx checked with the
dimorphodon.

"Just."

"Then let's get
moving," Teggs ordered. "I've
got a plan – but there's not a
moment to lose!"

The *Sauropod* was soon in secret orbit
around Geldos Beta. Arx, Iggy and
Teggs watched as Dasta's stolen shuttle
came into land. Then Teggs and Iggy
followed them down in the prison ship
at a safe distance.

"We'd better get after them fast," said

Teggs, stepping onto the planet's sandy surface. "As soon as they've got the replicator, they'll take off again."

Iggy nodded grimly. "And that could mean we lose Gipsy as well as the chance to get our bodies back!"

The two transformed astrosaurs scurried off through the sand in search of their real bodies. After a few minutes they reached a sand dune, and climbed to the very top.

"There we are," said Teggs quietly, peeking over the edge. "I mean, there *they* are. We've found them just in time!"

It was a strange feeling, watching themselves.

Dasta, the fake Teggs, was threatening Gipsy with his mighty tail. He swished it about impatiently. Gipsy was digging in the sand, while Ardul half-heartedly helped.

"Ugh," hissed Iggy. "I hate the feeling

of sand between my toes! Watching Ardul do that to my body is giving me shivers!"

"I couldn't stand it if my tail was used to hurt Gipsy," said Teggs softly. "In fact, my plan depends on Gipsy getting well clear of us – I mean, *them*."

Iggy nodded. "What we need is a distraction." Suddenly Ardul jumped high in the air. "We has found it!" he cried, excitedly. "The Sheep-Locator is right here!"

"*Replicator*, you ignoramus!" yelled Dasta. "You're right! There it is! Pull it out, girl, you stripy sausage! I must test it, right away."

Gipsy dragged a large, metal box from out of the sand. It looked like an oven with a big lever on the side and some flashing lights on top. "Doesn't look like much to me," she grunted.

"Prepare to be amazed," said Dasta.

Teggs and Iggy watched as he placed a single gold coin inside the replicator and

pulled the lever. The lights flashed
crazily, on and off, on and off – and
then the door swung open.

Gipsy gasped. The
replicator was *bulging*
with gold coins.

"It still works!"
cried Dasta in
delight. He grabbed
some of the coins with his mouth.
"Real gold! Ha! I'm rich! I'm rich!"

"That is where you is wrong," said
Ardul suddenly. He stomped forwards
and picked up the replicator. "Now you
has shown me how this machine works,
I is thinking I shall take it for myself."

"No!" gasped Dasta. "You – you
can't double-cross me!"

"Why not?" asked Ardul.

"Because I was going to double-cross
you first, that's why not!" Dasta raised
his tail. "Now put down the
replicator!"

"No," said Ardul. "I is going to take it away in that shuttle and be rich."

"Over my dead body!" cried Dasta.

Teggs gave Iggy a worried look. "Over *my* dead body, actually!"

"We're not just titchy little coelophysis any more, Ardul," said Dasta. "We're big, mean fighting machines. I could squash you with a swish of this tail!"

Ardul raised his iguanodon thumb spikes. "Or I could poke you with these and bring an ear to your tie."

"I think he means a *tear to your eye*, Dasta," said Gipsy, helpfully.

"I could do that too," Ardul agreed.

"We'll see," snarled Dasta. So saying, he whacked Ardul on the head with his tail!

Ardul staggered back and dropped the replicator on the sand. Then, with an angry hoot, he charged at Dasta and knocked him off his feet. Dasta responded by biting Ardul on the tail. Ardul yelped, and poked Dasta in the nose with his sharp thumb.

"Stop fighting, you two!" yelled Gipsy. "You wouldn't treat your own bodies like this, would you?"

"Ouch!" gasped Teggs, as Ardul brought a big rock crashing down on Dasta's head. "We've got to move fast, Iggy – before our bodies are battered to bits. Otherwise we'll be stuck as coelophysis for ever!"

Chapter Nine

A DEADLY GAMBLE

Dasta and Ardul's battle grew wilder. It was stegosaurus versus iguanodon in a furious fighting frenzy!

Ardul jabbed Dasta in the ribs with a karate chop. Dasta gave him a hefty kick with one enormous foot.

The two dinosaurs kept on fighting. Teggs and Iggy watched in amazement.

"I didn't know my body could do *that*!" gasped Iggy, as Ardul stood on his hands and slapped Dasta's face with his short, stiff tail.

"And I didn't know I could balance on my back!" cried Teggs, as Dasta spun backwards to get out of the way and whacked Ardul with his head. "I have to say, I'm picking up tips!"

"Look!" hissed Iggy. "They're so busy fighting they've forgotten about Gipsy!"

Gipsy had been left on her own with the replicator. "Break it up, you two!" she shouted at Dasta and Ardul. "Those aren't your bodies to bruise!"

"I'll go and get her," Teggs told Iggy. "You signal Arx. It's time to put the plan into action – now!"

With that Teggs raced over the top of

the dune. "Gipsy!" he cried. "Get out of there!"

Gipsy looked up, and gasped. It looked like a mean-looking coelophysis was rushing towards her, teeth bared! Her head-crest flushed red with anger, and she raised her fists, ready for a fight.

"It's all right, Gipsy!" the creature cried. "It's me, Teggs!"

"Teggs?" She peered closely at the scary animal. "Captain, is that really you?"

"Your favourite colour is orange, your mother's name is Doris and you

don't like cabbage,"
cried the coelophysis.

Gipsy grinned. "It *is*
you!"

"It certainly is,"
Teggs agreed. "Now,
pick up that replicator and let's get out
of here. NOW!"

"Yes, sir," she saluted.

Dasta and Ardul were blurs of speed
now as the battle raged on. Tails
thwacked. Heads clunked. Claws
scraped and feet stomped.

Teggs winced. "If
we ever *do* get
back in our
bodies, we'll be
aching for
weeks!"

Gipsy staggered
along beside him with
the replicator. Then a
dark shadow fell over them.

"The *Sauropod*!" she cried.

Sure enough, the huge, egg-shaped ship was swooping down from the skies above.

"Speed up, Gipsy," Teggs urged her. "We have to put as much distance between us and those carnivore crooks as we can!"

"Why?" panted Gipsy.

"Look out, you two!" cried Iggy. He dashed down and helped them up to the top of the sand dune. "Arx is ready for the big drop!"

"Iggy!" Gipsy dropped the replicator and gave him a massive hug. "Big drop? What do you mean?"

Teggs pointed. "He means *that*!"

The *Sauropod* stopped over the spot where Dasta and Ardul were still fighting. They were so busy bashing each other's brains out, they didn't notice a big pair of doors open above their heads. A second later, tons and

tons of plants and seeds came tumbling out – completely burying the dinosaurs and everything around them!

"Direct hit!" cheered Teggs. "That should stop those stupid crooks fighting for a while!"

"And save our bodies from an even bigger battering!" laughed Iggy.

Dasta's head appeared like a periscope through the sea of seeds. "I'm stuck!" he shouted.

"Me too!" spluttered Ardul, pushing his head out from a pile of plants.

"It's those astrosaurs," Dasta roared. "They've tricked us!"

"True," Teggs agreed with a smile. "Whatever body you're in, it's the *mind* that matters!"

The *Sauropod* landed at the bottom of the sand dune, and Arx came galloping out. Behind him, a flock of dimorphodon flapped about, holding the mind-swapper between them.

"That was a good plan, Captain," Arx smiled. "Now let's get mind-swapping before they dig themselves free!"

The astrosaurs waded through the

scattered seeds and plants to reach
Dasta and Ardul. "It's over, you two,"
said Teggs. "You're going back to your
old bodies — and back to prison!"

Dasta and Ardul struggled but the
food held them firm. The dimorphodon
dropped the helmets on their heads,
while Gipsy looked after Teggs and
Iggy.

"All set, Arx?" asked Teggs hopefully.

But Arx was still peering at the
mind-swapper's controls. "It's more
complicated than I thought it would
be."

"Of course it's complicated! It takes a *genius* to work it," said Dasta proudly. "You haven't a hope!"

Iggy scowled at him. "Tell us how it works!"

"Only if you promise to let me go," said Dasta slyly.

"We can't," Teggs told him. "You're too great a menace. Arx, I'm sorry, but you'll just have to work it out for yourself."

Suddenly Ardul started wiggling about. "While you is doing that, I is going to dig myself free!"

"Quick, Arx," cried Iggy.

"I *think* I can do it," said Arx nervously.

"If you get it wrong, you could fry our minds!" cried Dasta.

"We trust you, Arx," said Teggs. "Do it."

Arx looked at Gipsy. She nodded.

"Very well," he said, his horn hovering over a blue button.

"No!" gasped Dasta. "Not that one!"

"He's trying to trick you, Arx," said Teggs, gritting his teeth. "Do whatever you think is right. That's an order!"

Arx closed his eyes, made a wish and hit the button.

Chapter Ten

WHO'S WHO?!

The mind-swapper hummed and throbbed and crackled into life. Soon it was sucking up the dinosaurs' minds like milkshake.

Teggs gasped. His head felt on fire again.

Iggy felt the world spinning round and round . . .

"I just hope I've got this machine working properly," said Arx as it rattled and chugged behind him. "What if their minds end up in the wrong bodies? What if they get lost somewhere along the way?"

"You've done your best, Arx," said Gipsy. "Now we just have to hope!"

The mind-swapper sucked harder and harder. The noises it made grew louder and louder. And then it started to smoke. Pink sparks crackled all around it.

"I think it's overloading!" cried Arx. "Get down, Gipsy!"

The two astrosaurs threw themselves

to the ground. The dimorphodon flapped away into the sky.

The mind-swapper throbbed and spat and squelched and snorted . . . And then –

Boom! It exploded in a blaze of light.

"That's that, then," said Arx, getting back up.

"What if it didn't work?" asked Gipsy.

"Don't even think that!" he said.

The two coelophysis were asleep on the sand. Teggs' and Iggy's bodies lay still, half-buried by weeds and seeds.

Then the stegosaurus stirred. The iguanodon awoke.

Gipsy crossed her hooves. "Teggs? Iggy? Is that you?"

They looked at each other, in a daze.

"I ache all over . . . but I'm back!" yelled Teggs, and he gave a whoop of joy.

"Me too!" cheered Iggy. "We're back in our own bodies!"

"You did it, Arx!" Gipsy hugged him.

"I knew he wouldn't let us down!" beamed Teggs, bounding free of the plants and seeds.

"You're a hero, Arx!" said Iggy. "You deserve a medal!"

Arx blushed.

"Hold on a minute,"

said Teggs. "What about Dasta and Ardul?"

"Of course!" cried Iggy. "If they're back in their own bodies, there's nothing to stop them sneaking off!"

But the astrosaurs were too late. The two coelophysis had already gone.

"If only I'd watched them," moaned Gipsy.

The flock of dimorphodon flapped back down from the sky. One of them landed on Arx's nose and gave a loud squawk.

"This one has spotted them," said the triceratops. "He says they've sneaked off to your prison ship, Captain. They'll get away now, for sure!"

Teggs looked at Iggy and smiled. "Don't bet on it," he said.

Iggy grinned back. "You see, we left our guard dog on board."

"Guard dog?" Gipsy frowned.

Behind the big sand dune, a clanking, mechanical sound grew slowly louder. Arx and Gipsy cried out as a terrifying monster came into sight.

It was a robot T. rex!

It clutched Dasta in one mighty metal hand and Ardul in the other.

"Don't worry, he's a friend," Iggy explained. "He used to guard the prison, but I rewired him. I needed someone tall to fix the top of the ship!"

"He'll do anything we say," Teggs added. "And he'll certainly hold onto these two until the nearest space prison can pick them up!"

"Curse you, Teggs!" snarled Dasta.

"You is rotten as a raptor!" added Ardul.

"That's a point," said Arx. "We had a

run-in with raptors on the way here. What if we bump into them again on the way back?"

"Don't worry," said Teggs. "Once we've explained how we recaptured two of their most wanted criminals, they'll have to let us leave in peace."

"But what about the starving dinosaurs on Diplos?" asked Gipsy. "What are *they* going to do? We've dumped all their lovely food!"

"Simple," said Iggy. "We give them the replicator!"

Teggs nodded. "Put a single plant into that thing, and ten seconds later . . . out pop a hundred more!"

Arx smiled. "That will solve their food shortage overnight."

"And they'll never be hungry again," said Gipsy. "Brilliant!"

"So what are we waiting for?" said Iggy. "The sooner we deliver it, the better."

He picked up the replicator and set off back to the *Sauropod*. Arx followed, the dimorphodon flapping all around him.

But Gipsy held back. She could see that Teggs was looking at Dasta, still struggling in the grip of the robot T. rex.

"What a waste," he muttered.

Gipsy put a gentle hoof on his shoulder. "You mean . . . if only Dasta had used his brains to help people instead of making himself rich?"

He looked at her, puzzled. "No. I was just thinking – what a *waist*!" He smiled. "That sneaky coelophysis is a real skinny-ribs. It was quite nice to be slim and nimble for a change!"

Gipsy stared at him. "Don't tell me you'd rather be *him* than yourself!"

"No way," cried Teggs, striding off to the *Sauropod* after the others. "I'm the captain of the best ship in the Dinosaur Space Service, with the best crew in the universe. And I must be due another adventure any time now!" He looked back and gave Gipsy an enormous grin. "What could possibly be better than that?"

THE END

TALKING DINOSAUR!

STEGOSAURUS –
STEG-oh-SORE-us

HADROSAUR –
HAD-roh-sore

TRICERATOPS –
try-SERRA-tops

DIMORPHODON –
die-MORF-oh-don

IGUANODON –
ig-WA-noh-don

DIPLODOCUS –
di-PLOH-do-kus

COMPSOGNATHUS –
komp-soh-NAY-thus

COELOPHYSIS –
SEEL-oh-FIE-sis

ASTROSAURS
BOOK FIVE

THE SKIES OF FEAR

Read the first chapter here!

Chapter One

THE LONG SQUAWK

It was midnight on board the DSS *Sauropod*. All was quiet as the ship soared through space.

A few astrosaurs were working late. Ankylosaurs tinkered with the ship's mighty engines. The alarm pterosaur made a cup of swamp tea to help her stay awake.

And then a strange sound started up.

It was a weird, squawking, jittering sound. Like a T. rex trying to lay a two-ton egg. Like a thousand chickens singing from the bottom of a well. Like a billion beaks bashing at a battleship.

The sound blared from the *Sauropod*'s speakers all round the ship. The ankylosaurs dropped their tools in surprise. The alarm pterosaur screeched but no one could hear her over the dreadful din.

Captain Teggs jumped out of bed and galloped to the nearest lift, still in his pyjamas. For Teggs, the best things in life were eating and having adventures, ideally at the same time. But being woken at midnight by a sinister sound was enough to make even *him* lose his appetite.

As he reached the lift he saw that Gipsy had got there ahead of him. She took her hooves from her ears to salute him.

"Never mind that," Teggs told her. "If my hooves could *reach* my ears, I'd cover them too! We've got to stop that terrible noise!"

"I'm sure the dimorphodon are working out what's going on right now," said Gipsy.

The dimorphodon were the *Sauropod*'s flight crew. With their nimble claws and delicate beaks they worked the ship's controls swiftly and surely.

Or rather, they *usually* did.

As Teggs and Gipsy burst out of the lift and onto the flight deck, they found the dimorphodon were standing as still as statues.

"Quick, shut off the speakers," Teggs

told her. "I think my ears are about to explode!"

Gipsy rushed to her post and pressed a button. A sudden silence fell over the flight deck. Then the lift doors swished open and a green triceratops burst inside. It was Arx. He had dressed so quickly, he'd forgotten to take off his nightcap.

"Are we under attack?" he gasped.

"I don't know!" Teggs turned to Gipsy. "Any sign of enemy ships?"

"None, sir." She peered closely at her instruments. "The signal is coming from a long way away . . ."

"Try to get a fix on it," Teggs ordered. He was inspecting the dimorphodon. Their little eyes were goggly and glazed, and their beaks hung open.

"They're in some kind of trance," said Arx, sad to see his flapping friends in

127

such a state. "That sound – perhaps it's affected them!"

Just then, Iggy stomped out of the lift.

"I was having a brilliant dream about beating the raptors in a space-car race," he grumbled. "Then that nasty noise made me fall out of bed! What *was* it?"

"We're trying to find out," said Teggs, crossing to Gipsy's side. "But first I'd better talk to the crew!"

"Good idea," Iggy agreed. "After a scare like that, we'll have enough extra dung on board to power the ship for a whole month!"

Gipsy flicked a switch and Teggs's voice boomed over the rattling speakers. "This is your captain! Don't panic – we are not under attack."

But suddenly the flight crew snapped back into life. They squealed and squawked and flapped all around, working the controls at top speed.

"What's got into them?" gasped Gipsy.

The ground lurched beneath their feet. "We're changing course!" said Arx.

"Stop it!" shouted Teggs. "We're on our way to meet Admiral Rosso at DSS Headquarters! You can't just steer us somewhere else!"

But the dimorphodon wouldn't listen.

Read the rest of
THE SKIES OF FEAR
to find out where the *Sauropod* is being taken!

Find your fantastic **ASTROSAURS** collector cards in the back of this book. More cards available in each **ASTROSAURS** title. You can also add to your collection by logging on to

www.astrosaurs.co.uk